William Williams Documents

ELLIS ISLAND IMMIGRANTS

by Rebecca Rowell

Content Consultant

Vincent J. Cannato
Associate Professor of History
University of Massachusetts, Boston

Essential Library

An Imprint of Abdo Publishing | abdopublishing.com

abdopublishing.com

Published by Abdo Publishing, a division of ABDO, PO Box 398166, Minneapolis, Minnesota 55439. Copyright © 2018 by Abdo Consulting Group, Inc. International copyrights reserved in all countries. No part of this book may be reproduced in any form without written permission from the publisher. Essential Library™ is a trademark and logo of Abdo Publishing.

Printed in the United States of America, North Mankato, Minnesota
032017
092017

THIS BOOK CONTAINS
RECYCLED MATERIALS

Cover Photo: New York Public Library
Interior Photos: New York Public Library, 4, 6, 8, 10, 12–13, 14, 18, 19, 21, 25, 29, 32–33, 36, 38, 40–41, 43, 44–45, 49, 51, 53, 54, 56, 58–59, 62, 64–65, 70, 77, 78, 80, 83, 85, 88, 90, 99, 100 (top left), 100 (top middle), 100 (top right), 100 (bottom left), 100 (bottom right); Tony Baggett/ iStockphoto, 16–17; Fototeca Gilardi/Getty Images, 22; Red Line Editorial, 26–27; Bettmann/Getty Images, 31; Universal History Archive/UIG/ Getty Images, 68–69; Bettmann/Getty Images, 74; ullstein bild/Getty Images, 93; National Park Service, 94–95

Editor: Arnold Ringstad
Series Designer: Becky Daum

Publisher's Cataloging-in-Publication Data

Names: Rowell, Rebecca, author.
Title: William Williams documents Ellis Island immigrants / by Rebecca Rowell.
Description: Minneapolis, MN : Abdo Publishing, 2018. | Series: Defining images |
    Includes bibliographical references and index.
Identifiers: LCCN 2016962122 | ISBN 9781532110184 (lib. bdg.) |
    ISBN 9781680788037 (ebook)
Subjects: LCSH: United States--Emigration and immigration--History--Juvenile
    literature. | Immigrants--United States--History--Juvenile literature. | Ellis
    Island Immigration Station (N.Y. and N.J.)--History-- Juvenile literature. |
    Williams, William, 1862-1947--Juvenile literature. | Photographers-- United
    States--Juvenile literature.
Classification: DDC 325.73--dc23
LC record available at http://lccn.loc.gov/2016962122

CONTENTS

CHAPTER ONE

Taking Charge

President Theodore Roosevelt gave William Williams an important assignment when he appointed the lawyer commissioner of Ellis Island in 1902: make it respectable. The Ellis Island facility, the point of arrival for most immigrants to the United States, was barely ten years old. People were passing through the island by the thousands each day. During Williams's first week as commissioner, more than 25,000 immigrants entered Ellis Island's Great Hall for processing.[1]

The reputation of the immigration station, a beacon of hope for those seeking a new life in the United States, had become tarnished. Employees mistreated new arrivals. Many jobs at the facility were won through corrupt methods, and immigration laws

The main building at Ellis Island was easily visible to immigrants as they approached the facility from the water.

Williams played a key role in the US immigration system at a time when the country was welcoming huge numbers of immigrants.

were sometimes ignored. Roosevelt demanded improvements in all these areas. Williams arrived determined to do just that—and more.

Serving as Commissioner

In his position as head of the Ellis Island immigration processing facility, Williams had a double role. He had to get the facility in proper working order, making it as efficient as possible as workers processed the thousands of immigrants who graced its doorway every day. He also had to ensure his employees followed and enforced immigration laws established by the US government, which changed often and were becoming more restrictive in limiting who could enter the country.

Williams quickly got to work setting the nation's leading immigration center on a path to improvement. He planned to tackle the corruption and other problems that existed. He would leave his mark on the nation's first federal immigration center and affect the lives of many of the people who passed through the site.

Williams was meticulous. He kept a record of his time at Ellis Island, writing in a journal and saving newspaper clippings. He collected and preserved dozens of photographs of Ellis Island and the newly arrived immigrants there. Many of the photos were taken by the clerks who worked at the site. Some photos, such as images taken by professional photographer Edwin Levick, captured the island's grounds and facilities. Others were portraits of immigrants. Many of these were taken by Augustus F. Sherman, a clerk who worked at Ellis Island and one of the many people Williams supervised as commissioner. The subjects in Sherman's photographs were young and old, male and female. They were often clad in traditional clothing from their

WILLIAM WILLIAMS

William Williams was born in New London, Connecticut, on June 2, 1862. He came from an upper-class family that had a strong history in North America dating back to before the founding of the United States. A great-great-great-grandfather on his mother's side, Jonathan Edwards, was a prominent minister. Edwards was the leading theologian of British American Puritanism and played a role in the Great Awakening, a religious movement that took place in the mid-1700s. Williams had two prominent family members on his father's side as well. Robert Williams, a Puritan, helped settle Deerfield, Massachusetts. William Williams signed the Declaration of Independence as a representative from Connecticut.

Williams began college in Germany, but then enrolled at Yale University in his junior year. After graduating in 1884, he attended Harvard Law School. Williams got a degree in law in 1888 and went to work as a lawyer. In the 1890s, before becoming commissioner of Ellis Island, Williams worked as a corporate lawyer in New York City, where he had his own practice. He also held a position as a lawyer with the federal government, negotiating with the United Kingdom over the Bering Sea. That job had him working in Washington, DC, and in Paris, France. He returned to his New York law practice next, holding this position until becoming commissioner of Ellis Island in 1902.

Williams had gained extensive experience in legal and government matters before coming to Ellis Island.

homelands. All the photos give a glimpse into what Ellis Island was like in the early 1900s as people from across the ocean sought to make the United States their new home.

Joy and Anguish

Over the years, Ellis Island would become a symbol of hope for those who arrived by ship in New York Harbor. But it was also a site that caused fear and anxiety. Entry was not guaranteed. Many arrivals had to submit to physical and mental examination. Depending on the results, immigrants could be denied entry into the United States. Sometimes this meant they simply had to wait to overcome an illness or be claimed by someone already in the country. But some arrivals were deported and sent back to their homelands, their hopes dashed.

AUGUSTUS F. SHERMAN

Augustus F. Sherman was the source of many portraits in Williams's collection. Sherman was born in Pennsylvania in 1865. He moved to New York City in 1884 and began working as a clerk at Ellis Island in 1892. He advanced to senior clerk and sometimes served on boards of special inquiry. These boards heard individual cases of detainees, listening to witnesses and deciding if the detainees would be allowed into the country.

Sherman was a self-taught photographer. He may have started photography as a result of knowing Terence V. Powderly, who served as commissioner general of immigration from 1897 to 1902. Because of his position as clerk at Ellis Island, Sherman had access to the site and the thousands of people who arrived there every week.

Sherman died on February 16, 1925. In the 1960s, Mary Sherman Peters, his niece, donated the remainder of the photos by her uncle to the American Immigration Museum. This facility is now called the Ellis Island Museum of Immigration.

Inspections helped immigration officials decide whether newly arrived people would be welcomed into the country or sent back home.

Inspectors rejected immigrants for a variety of reasons. Some were physical, such as carrying an infectious disease. Some were mental. Testers had immigrants arrange blocks to check their intelligence. Other rejections had to do with good character and not having been in prison. Many were based on stereotypes and reflected prejudice.

As the United States progressed in a world that was becoming ever more industrial, immigration officials sought to bring in young, strong, capable people to aid the nation's advancement. Williams believed in that goal. He had firm ideas about who should be allowed to enter the United States and who should not. He felt arrivals had to be able to work and care for themselves.

In its six decades of operation, Ellis Island welcomed millions of foreigners who would

EDWIN LEVICK

Several photos among those Williams kept while serving as commissioner of Ellis Island were taken by Edwin Levick. Levick was born in London, England, in 1869. He spent some of his childhood in Asia and the Middle East. He also studied in France. Levick moved to the United States in 1899. He acquired a love of the water and sailboats as a child and would gain a reputation as a marine photographer, especially of boat races. He photographed other sports as well, including golf, horse racing, polo, and tennis. Levick's photos of Ellis Island that feature the harbor and barges reflect his specialty in marine photography. The award-winning photographer ventured outside his standard subjects when he shot immigrants in various stages of being processed, such as the medical inspection line. Levick died on November 26, 1929.

become Americans. Approximately 40 percent of US citizens today can trace at least one relative to Ellis Island.[2] During the site's heyday in the early 1900s, Williams used his position as commissioner to improve processes and procedures. He also set the standards for what made a new arrival acceptable. But Williams did more than that. In his photo collection, he documented a unique part of US history and preserved special moments in people's lives. The newly arrived individuals in these portraits have become the faces of Ellis Island.

CHAPTER TWO

Immigration to America

Soon after Ellis Island opened its doors, its empty halls would begin filling with waves upon waves of immigrants.

When Williams became commissioner of Ellis Island in 1902, the United States was in the middle of an immigration boom. Ellis Island was the first federal immigration station in the United States. When the site opened its doors in 1892, the federal government had only just begun overseeing immigration, forming the Office of Superintendent of Immigration a year earlier. Before that time, individual states had overseen immigration and were supposed to enforce federal immigration legislation. Federal oversight was new, but people had been arriving in America for centuries.

People began immigrating to North America long before the United States was a nation.
In 1607, approximately 100 people from England established Jamestown, the first English
colony in North America, in what is now Virginia.[1] The Pilgrims, who sailed from England
seeking religious freedom in America, arrived in 1620.

Immigration Booms

Initially, after the United States became a nation in 1776, immigration was relatively light.
Poverty changed that. People in Europe and elsewhere set their sights on the new country,
which many believed held the promise for greater economic opportunities and less repression
because of its constitutional freedoms. Almost 600,000 immigrants arrived in the 1830s.
That number almost tripled in the 1840s, with nearly 1.75 million arrivals.[2] Ships brought
immigrants to several ports, including Boston, Massachusetts; Charleston, South Carolina;
Philadelphia, Pennsylvania; and San Francisco, California. Most landed in New York, New York.
Dozens of ships cruised into New York Harbor each day in the early 1840s, carrying as many as
1,000 immigrants each.[3]

During this era, a few groups in particular came in great numbers. From 1814 to 1844, one million Irish people arrived in the United States. In 1845, Ireland began experiencing a famine that persisted for several years. A blight devastated the potato crop, the staple of the Irish diet.

An Ellis Island portrait of a young girl from Rättvik, Sweden

Without it, people suffered terribly and fled for survival. In the 1850s, approximately one million more Irish immigrants arrived in the United States.[4] Similar to the Irish, many Germans left their homeland to escape poverty. By 1860, people from Ireland and Germany together made up 70 percent of the population of immigrants in the United States.[5]

A Time of Transition

Ellis Island opened during a time of transition in US immigration. The number of arrivals from Ireland and Germany had decreased dramatically, but the overall number of arrivals did not drop. Rather, more people came from other parts of Europe. In 1860, people from northern countries such as Denmark, Norway, and Sweden moved to the United States. By 1920, almost two million Scandinavians had traveled across the Atlantic.[6] Many people emigrated from the eastern and southern regions of Europe, too. This was particularly so when Williams became commissioner. Jews were fleeing hardship in Russia and Eastern Europe. In 1910, approximately 484,000 Jewish immigrants made their way to Ellis Island.[7] Other groups from Eastern Europe that arrived in large numbers included Czechs, Hungarians, Poles, Serbs, and Slovaks. Many Greeks and Italians came to America from Southern Europe.

An Ellis Island portrait of a man from Algeria

Immigrants also came from beyond Europe. Residents of Armenia, Syria, and Turkey emigrated from their homelands in the Middle East to escape problems such as famine, religious persecution, and war. Many photos in Williams's collection show these new immigrants. Portraits by Sherman highlight how varied immigrants were, from a young Swedish girl in her blouse, skirt, apron, and hat, to an old Danish man who looks like a sea captain, to a young Algerian man in a turban and a long robe. For all these immigrants, their first exposure to the United States would be at the Ellis Island immigration station.

CASTLE GARDEN

The first official immigration center in the United States was run by New York State. Called Castle Garden, it was located in the Battery, a 25-acre (10 ha) waterfront park in Manhattan. Castle Garden operated from 1855 to 1890.[8] It was meant to provide immigrants a haven from con artists, thieves, and others who preyed on them. But the site became the opposite of a sanctuary. The abundance of arrivals led to overcrowding. In the center's 35 years of operation, more than eight million immigrants passed through its doors.[9] Workers did not always do a good job conducting medical inspections, and government officials worried about disease. Even with these issues, Castle Garden made important strides in immigration that continued at Ellis Island, including establishing medical inspections. The center also allowed immigrants to exchange their money for American currency and purchase train tickets. Today, Castle Garden is the main landmark at the Battery and is now called Castle Clinton National Monument.

CAPTURING THE HUDDLED MASSES

Peter Mesenhöller, a cultural anthropologist who specializes in still photography and immigration studies, has studied Sherman's photographs: "The technical procedures in those days were very difficult. You had these huge tripod cameras and the exposure took how many seconds, and you had to get the lighting just right and have your subjects sit perfectly still. And with an average of about 5,000 people each day coming through Ellis Island at peak times, it must have been quite an undertaking."[10]

Sherman photographed his subjects outdoors and indoors. He positioned immigrants in outdoor photographs in places where he could use natural light. Popular spots included a balcony, the lawn, or the roof.

When photographing indoors, Sherman used either sheets or screens from medical exam rooms as backdrops, and he was more careful with poses. When he photographed people's faces directly, he had them look into the camera. For three-quarter portraits, they looked into the distance. Subjects held up their chins and kept their shoulders relaxed. Facial expressions were often relaxed as well, and some people even smiled. This is often not the case in his group photographs, where expressions are usually more serious or even sad.

Ellis Island photographers took advantage of natural light when possible.

CHAPTER THREE

The Journey to Ellis Island

Ellis Island began as a pile of sand in the Hudson River. The Mohegans, a Native American tribe, called the island Kioshk, or Gull Island. In the 1630s, Dutchman Michael Pauw bought the island. He renamed it Oyster Island because of the abundance of oysters there. Later, in the 1700s, people began calling it Gibbet Island. The gibbets, or gallows, on Gibbet Island were specifically for hanging men found guilty of piracy.

Around the time of the American Revolutionary War (1775–1783), merchant Samuel Ellis owned the small piece of land. He established

In the nation's early years, the port of New York City was a major hub of activity.

a tavern there for fishermen. Ellis died in 1794, but his family kept the island until 1808, when the state of New York bought it for $10,000.[1] The US War Department paid the state of New York for use of the island, which soon had military fortifications that were active in the War of 1812 (1812–1815) and the American Civil War (1861–1865). The US government did not use the island again until it took over immigration oversight from the states.

Preparing for Immigration

In 1890, the federal government allotted $75,000 to create the first federal immigration processing center on the island.[2] Considerable work was needed to develop the site. First, workers added enough landfill around the island's edge to double its size. Some of this dirt and rock came from digging tunnels for New York's subways. Other work on the island included erecting buildings and adding a dock. The project also involved creating a channel that would allow large ships to navigate through the harbor and reach the island.

On January 1, 1892, 700 immigrants arrived at Ellis Island's new immigration processing center.[3] The site operated for more than five years. Then, disaster struck. On June 15, 1897, a fire destroyed the facility's main building. Two hundred immigrants were on the island at the time.[4]

Many of the immigration facility's structures were built upon artificially expanded portions of the island.

The Development of Ellis Island

Ellis Island is located in New York Harbor, near the island of Manhattan and Liberty Island, the location of the Statue of Liberty. Today, Ellis Island measures 27.5 acres (11.1 ha), but it began at only 3.5 acres (1.4 ha).[5] Adding landfill over many decades increased the island's size to what it is today.

The first expansion of Ellis Island occurred in the 1890s. A major building project enlarged the island's area to 14 acres (6 ha) by 1897. Over the next two decades, Ellis Island grew even more. This period of expansion was the island's biggest. Williams was commissioner during this time.

Although Ellis Island is a single island, its three parts are referred to as islands. Island One is the northern part. It includes the original island. The primary immigration facilities are here, including the main building. Islands Two and Three exist because of landfill. Medical buildings are located on them.

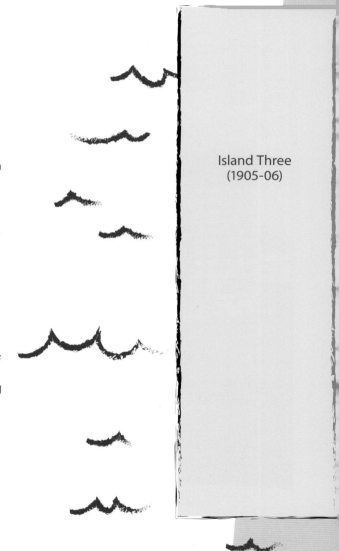

Island Three
(1905-06)

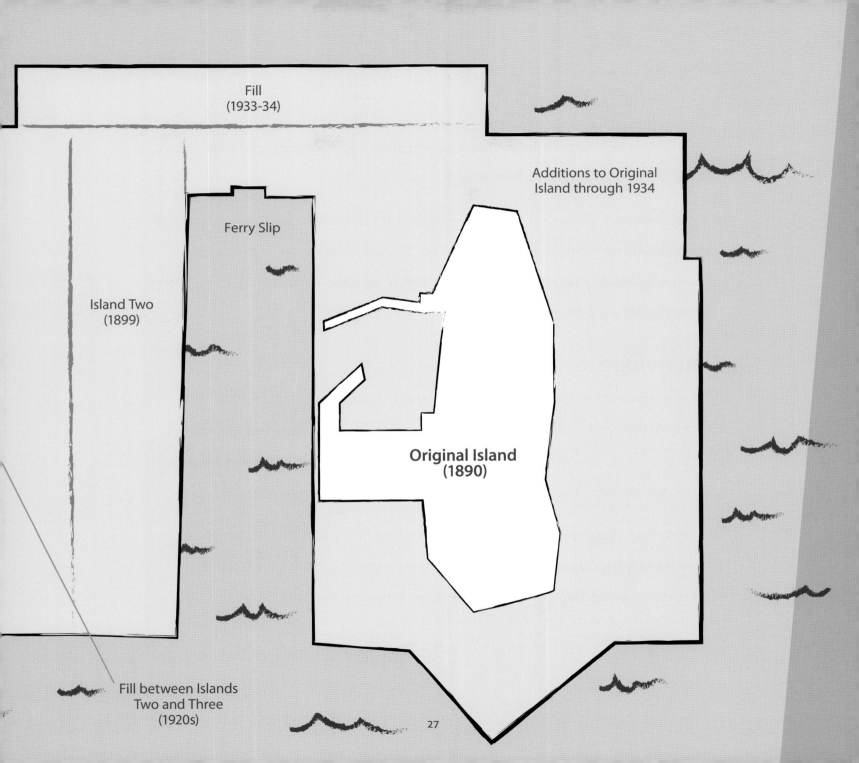

Fill
(1933-34)

Additions to Original
Island through 1934

Ferry Slip

Island Two
(1899)

Original Island
(1890)

Fill between Islands
Two and Three
(1920s)

27

None of them were hurt, but the fire destroyed immigration records going back decades. Much of this priceless information was forever lost.

While workers built a new processing center, the United States processed immigrants at the Barge Office, a site in Manhattan's Battery Park. Ellis Island reopened in December 1900. The new facility's first day was even busier than the first day at the old facility, with immigration workers processing 2,251 arrivals.[6]

Surviving Steerage

Traveling to the United States from Europe in a steamship took seven to ten days.[7] The conditions travelers experienced varied. Those with a first-class ticket could have a nice trip, as could those with a second-class ticket. These passengers often stayed in cabins with a bed, clean sheets, and blankets. They usually received good food, and the ship's crew treated them well.

But not everyone could afford to travel in such relative luxury. A majority of immigrants could buy only the cheapest tickets. That placed them in steerage. The space was crowded, with people crammed together in an open area, rather than assigned to a private room.

After overseas journeys on large ships, passengers transferred to smaller ferries to reach Ellis Island.

And there was no place for luggage and other belongings, so passengers had to store their items as best they could. Instead of beds with clean sheets, passengers had what could barely pass for mattresses—burlap bags stuffed with seaweed or straw. Temperatures in steerage could be uncomfortably hot or cold, depending on the season, and the food was bad. In addition, there were unwanted pests, such as rats. Another issue was sanitation and disease. Bathrooms and water were lacking in quantity and quality, which contributed to the spread of illnesses.

One ailment many steerage passengers experienced was seasickness. Vomiting was common, especially when waters were rough because of a storm. The result could be quite unpleasant. An immigrant described his experience in these conditions: "Hundreds of people had vomiting fits. I wanted to escape from that inferno but no sooner had I thrust my head forward from the lower bunk than someone above me vomited straight upon my head."[8]

The poor conditions in steerage took a toll on some passengers. Children were particularly susceptible to diseases spread there. Ellis Island records from 1907 reported that "1,506 children have been received at this station afflicted with measles, diphtheria, and scarlet fever, all of which diseased are due, more or less, to overcrowding and insanitary conditions. Of this number, 205 died."[9]

IMPROVED STEERAGE CONDITIONS

With time, conditions in steerage improved. Major advances happened in the 1910s. The changes were at least partly due to money. The companies that owned the ships wanted passengers and their money. By improving the accommodations, food, and general service they provided, companies became more appealing to immigrants. Some newer ships did not even have a steerage area. In its place were cabins big enough for four or six people. The rooms were small and simple, but they were a vast improvement over steerage. Some companies even provided dishes and utensils for these passengers to use.

Even with such improvements on some ships, many immigrants still traveled in the uncomfortable and poor conditions of steerage. That was because shipping lines continued to use their old ships alongside their newer ones.

These uncomfortable conditions were not limited to poor-quality ships. Luxury liners often had awful conditions, too. Edward Steiner, an immigrant and an immigrant advocate, wrote about such a ship, the *Kaiser Wilhelm II*:

Crowding and discomfort were common aboard ships loaded with immigrants bound for the United States.

> *There is neither breathing space below nor deck room above, and the 900 steerage passengers . . . are positively packed like cattle. On the whole, the steerage of the modern ship ought to be condemned as unfit for the transportation of human beings.*[10]

Having endured such an unpleasant experience traversing the Atlantic Ocean, immigrants were often elated to see the Statue of Liberty and then Ellis Island in New York Harbor. They had finally made it. But they had not yet completed their journey. They still had to be processed.

The Ellis Island immigration station awaited, managed under the watchful eye of Williams.

Becoming Commissioner

Williams's journey to Ellis Island was an unexpected one. The 39-year-old bachelor lawyer was

not looking to hold a political office and did not know Roosevelt, so when Williams received

a telegram from the president to have lunch at the White House in spring 1902, it was likely

a surprise.

Roosevelt wanted to clean up the nation's leading immigration processing center. He had

been searching for just the right candidate to take on the job as commissioner. Williams had

qualities that appealed to the president. He was wealthy and well educated, had a respectable

family background, and was a Republican who believed in reform, just as Roosevelt did.

During lunch, Roosevelt spoke with Williams for an hour. He wanted him to take on the

job immediately. Williams asked for time to consider the offer. He also asked Roosevelt why

he should accept the opportunity. Roosevelt described the job as one of the most interesting

ones he had the power to offer. Williams returned home to New York and mulled over the job, studying immigration law. He decided to accept the position. He started his job as commissioner of Ellis Island in April 1902.

The problems Roosevelt wanted addressed were clearly visible to the new commissioner. He noted in a journal entry, "The conditions as I found them when I took office have been frequently described. Immigrants were abused and maltreated and the whole building was filthy. Many corrupt inspectors were in office."[11]

Williams knew this was in part due to preceding commissioners, who were bad at their jobs and dishonest. Williams was careful to set a tone quite unlike his predecessors. He was not corrupt and would not tolerate corruption. He also expected quality work and humane

WILLIAMS CHANGES THE LANDSCAPE

As commissioner, Williams seemed to leave no stone unturned in his efforts to improve Ellis Island. This included landscaping. The *New York Times* even reported on his influence on the grounds. Before Williams was commissioner, "there was not a flower or a bush of any kind on the island." But by the summer of 1903, Ellis Island was a "well-regulated and unusually prettily decorated part."[12]

Williams changed the landscape through architecture, too, and it was to benefit immigrants. He had a steel canopy built, stretching from the dock where immigrants arrived to the front of the main building, where immigrants were processed. The canopy had a glass roof that shielded the immigrants from rain and wind.

treatment of all immigrants who made their way to Ellis Island. He made this expectation known clearly and quickly as he took on his new role.

Even with all his efforts to improve Ellis Island and the treatment of immigrants, Williams continued to have a generally low opinion of immigrants. In 1903, after serving as commissioner for one year, Williams noted seeing "a particularly undesirable stream of immigration."[13] He responded by focusing on keeping out the people deemed undesirable, particularly those immigrants he felt might end up needing public aid.

VOICING HIS DISLIKE OF IMMIGRANTS

Williams did not let his position as commissioner of Ellis Island stop him from voicing his dislike of immigrants—or at least his desire to be more careful about who should be allowed into the country. In January 1903, Williams spoke to the Federation of Churches and Christian Organizations:

I am sure it will not be sufficiently far reaching to touch the real evils of the existing immigration, [but] no further specific test other than the illiteracy test appears to be practicable as a means of keeping out undesirable immigrants. . . . Aliens have no inherent right to come here, and if the American people, as I think it does, wishes to exclude from the country generally undesirable people . . . and those who will be obviously unfit for American citizenship, I fail to see why they should not do so."[14]

CHAPTER FOUR

Island of Hope, Island of Tears

The main hall of the immigration station on Ellis Island was one of the first stopping points for vast numbers of immigrants to the United States.

When Williams took over managing Ellis Island, he was in charge of the main immigration center in the United States at a time when the US government was trying to exert stricter control over the immigration process. As a result, he and other officials had tremendous power to dictate who was allowed to enter the country.

In 1903, the year after Williams became commissioner, the federal government moved immigration oversight from the US Treasury Department to the Department of Commerce and Labor. With the move, the Immigration Bureau saw itself in a new light.

It would make immigration more centralized, controlled by officials in Washington, DC. It saw itself more as a business, and Williams, with his law background and focus on practicality and structure, was a good fit.

Reaching New York Harbor

Arriving at New York Harbor was no guarantee of a new life in America. For some immigrants, their moment of joy at reaching the United States would quickly turn to despair upon learning they were being deported to their homeland.

When a ship reached the harbor, the experiences of the immigrant passengers varied, at least initially. Those who had traveled in the first and second classes had to meet with a medical officer for a quick exam. Inspectors also checked information from these passengers against the information in the ship's log. An aid worker described a visit by an Ellis Island doctor:

> As quickly as possible, the little doctor, who was working for the public Health Service, would climb up and down a ladder on those ships that came in—he worked very, very hard. Sometimes they had to meet a ship at two or three o'clock in the morning.[1]

With the initial exams completed, officials allowed healthy travelers to proceed to wherever they desired. Those who had medical issues boarded barges to Ellis Island, along with all passengers in steerage.

Immigrants regularly had to wait to be processed. The length of the wait varied. So did the location. Sometimes, the wait was on the ship. If they arrived in the harbor in middle of the night, passengers needing processing would have to wait until morning to get to the island. Sometimes, immigrants were stuck on the barges, which were usually crowded. For example, a barge that arrived at noon would have to wait until 2:00 p.m. to unload. That is when the doctors and other personnel would return from lunch. Those stuck on a barge were provided with whatever food the barge had. This might be bread and sardines. Beverages included coffee

Levick's panoramic shot of the immigration station shows off the building's distinct architecture.

and milk. Levick's wide shot of the immigration station with a boat docked in front gives a sense of the repeated daily occurrence of barges arriving. To the right of the main building, the New York City skyline is barely visible in the distance.

Entering Ellis Island

Stepping onto Ellis Island, passengers were directed to the Great Hall for processing. Levick captured both the exterior and the interior of the building in some of his photographs. One shows the entrance to the facility, which has many windows and is lined with bushes. Immigrants entered it with all they brought with them to start a new life. They were met with a series of metal holding pens. Sherman snapped at least one photo of this area from a balcony. The seats below were filled to capacity with newly arrived immigrants waiting to be processed. English author H. G. Wells wrote about this part of Ellis Island in 1906 in *The Future in America: A Search after Realities*:

> All day long, through an intricate series of metal pens, the long procession [of new immigrants] files, step by step, bearing bundles and trunks and boxes, past this examiner and that, past the quick, alert medical officers, the tallymen and the clerks. At every point

immigrants are being picked out and set aside for further medical examination, for further questions, for the busy little courts; but the main procession satisfies conditions, passes on. It is a daily procession that, with a yard [0.9 m] of space to each, would stretch over three miles [4.8 km].[2]

Many arrivals wore the traditional garb of their homelands. For instance, some Dutch children wore shoes that came to an upturned point, and a German man wore his lederhosen, or leather shorts with suspenders. Sherman photographed hundreds of newly arriving immigrants.

A FLOOD OF PEOPLE

Frank Martocci was an employee at Ellis Island in 1907, its busiest year. He worked as an inspector and as an interpreter. He described a busy scene there: "Here, in the main building, they were lined up—a motley crowd in colorful costumes, all ill at ease and wondering what was to happen to them. . . . From nine o'clock in the morning to nine in the evening, we were continuously examining aliens. . . . I thought it was a stream that would never end. Every twenty-four hours from three to five thousand people came before us, and I myself examined four to five hundred a day. We were simply swamped by that human tide."[3]

The Line Inspection

Immigrants faced long lines. Workers who would determine if a person was fit for entry had to assess every arrival. The assessment included physical exams and interviews.

Immigrants faced multiple physical exams. Doctors employed by the US Public Health

Levick's photo of the immigration station's entrance shows off some of the landscaping Williams insisted upon adding to the island.

Service performed them. An initial exam took place in line. Doctors studied every immigrant who progressed slowly toward the Registry Room. This line inspection was fast, and doctors used it to look for obvious signs of disease and any evidence of what they considered mental or physical weakness. One Levick photo shows a family in line for the initial medical inspection, passing through a line defined by metal railings, making their route through immigration processing clear.

For immigrants who were flagged for potential medical issues during the brief line inspection, a second, more thorough exam took place in a separate room. The Ellis Island doctors were particularly concerned about identifying illnesses that were contagious, including tuberculosis. A skin disease common at that time, favus, was another focus. Doctors feared an immigrant with such an illness could cause an epidemic if he or she were allowed to enter the United States.

Another contagious disease that concerned officials was trachoma. It affects the eyes and can cause blindness. All immigrants had their eyes inspected, and the experience was quite painful for some. Checking the eye required lifting the eyelid. Some doctors used their fingers.

Others used a hairpin or a small metal tool called a buttonhook. An eye exam in which the inspector used a buttonhook was particularly painful. This upset many immigrants, particularly those whose children had to endure the pain.

Some travelers suffered from illnesses they had contracted during their trip. The poor conditions in steerage resulted in the spread of diseases such as measles and diphtheria. Doctors knew about the rough experience many immigrants had traveling in steerage, and they gave immigrant patients a chance to get well before performing a final medical exam. Doing this increased the chance a person who arrived sick would be allowed to enter the country.

When a doctor suspected a medical issue with an immigrant, he or she wrote on the

HOSPITALIZING IMMIGRANTS

Many immigrants who arrived at Ellis Island in need of medical care received treatment at one of the immigration center's hospitals. The US government built a hospital in 1902. It initially treated as many as 120 patients. The number grew to 275. In 1906, the hospital treated 7,464 patients, 2,794 of whom were children. Of the almost 7,500 patients treated in that year, 268 children and 59 adults died.[4]

Ellis Island got another hospital in 1907 when the government built a facility to treat people suffering from mental illness. It was called the Psychopathic Pavilion. The government built a third hospital, the Contagious Disease Hospital, in 1911. Specific areas of the hospital were set up for certain diseases, such as measles or trachoma. The hospital had space for 450 patients.

The doctors on Ellis Island encountered diseases from around the world. As a result, they gained valuable knowledge. If needed, they consulted with specialists. Public health care today follows practices Ellis Island started.

person's clothing with chalk. A letter signified the possible problem. For example, *B* was short for back, *F* was for face, and *H* was for heart. People who were marked in this way were pulled from the line for further inspection. This was done in an examination room. Immigrants who were clearly sick went to another location on the island: the Ellis Island Hospital.

While the work Ellis Island's doctors did could ultimately lead to a person being denied entry into the United States, these workers did not actually deny or admit immigrants. US immigrant inspectors made the final decisions.

Early on, Williams saw a problem with the inspection process. Only two months after assuming the role of commissioner, he made his first annual report. In it, he noted inspectors were not consistent in their work, marking some immigrants to be held based on ship records rather than as a result of an actual inspection. Williams suggested at least some inspectors

WILLIAMS AND THE MEDIA

As commissioner, Williams used the media to showcase the improvements at Ellis Island. He gave journalists stories. Williams also corrected facts writers got wrong. Williams wrote in a scrapbook an entry he titled "My Experiences with the Press." He explained in the entry: "I made great use of the press to accomplish my ends, which were to disseminate full and correct information as to what was going on at this office, the work of which affected the country in vital particulars, and in this I succeeded because I made Ellis Island an open book."[5]

were looking to make money from immigrants who might pay them to get into the country: "The fact that most of those marked were able-bodied people with large amounts of money are points not without interest."[6] He refused to tolerate such poor and dishonest work. He noted in his journal, "I shall use every means at my disposal to put an end to such criminal carelessness and disregard of United States laws."[7] To improve the inspection process, he told the inspectors to inspect all arrivals thoroughly and to the same degree.

Mental and Intelligence Assessments

Sometimes, immigrants were removed from the line inspection to undergo mental testing. Exclusions for mental reasons were many and varied. Some immigrants were denied entry because they were deemed not smart enough and were diagnosed as idiots, imbeciles, or morons—labels once used by medical professionals that are unacceptable today. These labels represented different mental ages. A person diagnosed as an idiot was considered three years old mentally, a person diagnosed as an imbecile was considered three to seven years old mentally, and a person diagnosed as a moron was considered eight to twelve years old mentally.

An immigrant, *right*, is interviewed by three Ellis Island staff members.

Other mental diagnoses that led to an immigrant being denied entry included being depressed, being an alcoholic, and having delusions or murderous thoughts. Officials also banned epileptics, those who suffer from seizures.

Officials used different methods to test immigrants' mental state and intelligence. They asked questions or had immigrants count forward and backward, arrange blocks or forms in a certain manner, take memory tests, or name different animals.

Doctors might test a person more than once. This was sometimes the case because they knew a poor mental rating on the initial test might be due to the stressful journey to the United States. In such instances, the official would wait a few days before testing the arrival again to give that person time to calm down. Passing a test required accuracy and speed. Doctors also considered how a person looked while taking a test. Failing a test did not automatically mean a person would be deported. Prospective immigrants had to do poorly on multiple tests before officials would officially exclude them.

Meeting with Inspectors

After being examined medically, new arrivals met with inspectors. These workers asked a variety of questions, including the person's age and sex, whether he or she was married, and his or her occupation. Inspectors asked for additional information as well, wanting to know if the person had family already in the United States and how much money the person was carrying. Inspectors also queried arrivals about criminal history, wanting to know if the person had ever been in prison. They asked immigrants if they had ever needed public assistance to survive. The inspectors were looking to weed out any newcomers who might become criminals in the

GETTING THE SHOT

Lewis W. Hine photographed immigrants at Ellis Island in 1905, around the same time Sherman was making his own portraits. Hine described the experience trying to take photos at the bustling immigration center: "We are elbowing our way thro[ugh] the mob at Ellis trying to stop the surge of bewildered beings oozing through the corridors, up the stairs and all over the place, eager to get it all over and be on their way. Here is a small group that seems to have possibilities so we stop 'em and explain in pantomime that it would be lovely if they would stick around just a moment. The rest of the human tide swirls around, often not too considerate of either the camera or us. We get the focus . . . then, hoping they will stay put, get the flash lamp ready. . . . Meantime, the group had strayed around a little." Hine described the skills required to manage the situation: "It took all the resources of a hypnotist, a supersalesman and a ball pitcher to prepare them to play the game then outguess them so most were not either wincing or shutting their eyes when the time came to shoot."[8]

Getting large groups to all look at the camera proved to be a challenge for Hine and other Ellis Island photographers.

United States or rely on the government for help. These immigrants were not allowed into the United States. Some were merely detained, held on Ellis Island a short time before being allowed to continue into the country. Others faced a harsher fate. They were deported.

Humane Treatment

Williams was quick to focus on improving the treatment of Ellis Island's immigrants. In his second month as commissioner, Williams let his employees know how they should treat immigrants. He posted a notice throughout Ellis Island's main building:

> *Immigrants must be treated with kindness and consideration. Any Government official violating the terms of this notice will be recommended for dismissal from the Service. Any other person so doing will be forthwith required to leave Ellis Island. It is earnestly requested that any violation hereof, or any instance of any kind of improper treatment of immigrants at Ellis Island, or before they leave the Barge Office, be promptly brought to the attention of the Commissioner.[9]*

Williams did not post the notice to serve simply as a scare tactic. He meant what he wrote and followed up on it when needed, addressing specific employees about their behavior. For example, he suspended John Bell, a gateman, for two weeks for using "vulgar and abusive language."[10] To another employee whose behavior he did not like, Williams sent a note:

I was very much displeased at the rough and unkind manner in which I heard you address two immigrants to the Discharging Bureau this afternoon. Do not let this occur again.[11]

Williams would continue to make changes and enforce his policies to improve the processes of the nation's top immigration processing center. Employees were to treat immigrants kindly, whether they were there a few hours, a few days, a few weeks, or longer.

Williams expected his employees to treat immigrants humanely and professionally.

CHAPTER FIVE

Detained, Deported

For the relatively small number of arrivals at Ellis Island who were not allowed entry into the country, two possible fates remained. They were either detained or deported. Neither option would be a pleasant experience.

Some immigrant women had a more difficult time gaining entry into the United States because they were seen as requiring more care and protection than men. Women also had limited employment opportunities, and the few jobs they were able to get paid less than those held by men. As a result, women were less likely to be able to

Women often faced more challenges as immigrants than their male counterparts.

Sherman photographed a pair of young Dutch children upon their arrival at the immigration station.

support themselves. Immigration officials felt they would be more likely to rely on public assistance, or that they might even turn to prostitution. Either outcome was unacceptable to officials.

In the first decade of the 1900s, US immigration policy focused heavily on keeping people out of the country if they might become public charges. Approximately 63 percent of immigrants who were denied entry were kept out of the country for this reason.[1] Because the government wanted to avoid accepting people who might need public aid, single mothers had a particularly difficult time gaining entry into the country. Inspectors rejected women who were unmarried and who had children born out of wedlock. These individuals, officials believed, posed a moral risk to the nation.

Women who arrived with only their children could enter on one condition. They had to show a relative was waiting for them. Many single mothers waited for this person to arrive and pick them up. Some of these women waited for days. If officials could not locate a woman's sponsor, they sent her back to her home country.

In addition to single mothers, officials singled out the elderly as likely to become what they called public charges—people who needed welfare or assistance to survive. Other groups included the sick and those considered mentally challenged. Journalist Jacob Riis wrote about Ellis Island's detainees in 1903:

ELLIS ISLAND'S FACILITIES

The Great Hall stands out as Ellis Island's main structure because authorities processed immigrants there. But the immigration center had many more facilities. Three hospitals treated various physical and mental illnesses, including contagious diseases. Ellis Island also had a laundry building. Workers there cleaned thousands of items each day. The laundry building also held a boiler room, where the furnace was located, an autopsy room, and a morgue. The island had a power station as well.

Here are the old, the stricken, waiting for friends able to keep them; the pitiful little colony

of women without the shield of a man's name in their hour of greatest need; the young

and pretty and thoughtless, for whom one sends up a silent prayer of thanksgiving. . . . And

the hopelessly bewildered are there, often enough exasperated at the restraint, which they

cannot understand.[2]

Detained

Approximately one-fifth of the immigrants who entered the Great Hall were detained there

temporarily.[3] Detainees stayed in dormitories on the third floor of the main building, above

the Great Hall where processing took place. One side of the floor was for men. The other

was for women and children. Accommodations were minimal. There was a bathroom and

some sinks with water, and detainees slept on bunk beds. The beds did not have mattresses.

Rather, they were simple cots with heavyweight fabric attached to metal frames. Each cot had

a blanket. The dormitories were usually packed with other detainees. Williams commented

on these facilities in 1911: "When all of the beds are occupied, as frequently they are, the

congestion in this room is very great, and since it has only an easterly exposure the temperature on summer nights may be 100 [degrees Fahrenheit (38°C)]."[4]

Immigrants who were detained also received food and had the opportunity to attend religious services. Children could attend a school, though they were not required to. Each day, school workers went to detention areas and asked children there if they wanted to attend. Those who agreed were usually between the ages of 10 and 14. Classes ranged from crafts to singing to learning English and studying the United States. The school had a playground on its roof, and children attending school would sometimes have an afternoon snack of milk and graham crackers.

Adults had their own opportunities to socialize and learn. Beginning in the 1910s, they could take part in a variety of activities, including concerts, movies, sports, and classes. Classes addressed topics such as knitting,

TESTING THE TESTS

Child detainees who attended school on Ellis Island did more than sing, learn English, and participate in other classes. They also took some of the processing center's psychological tests. Officials were hoping to discover which tests would be best to use on immigrants in general. Because not all immigrants spoke or read English, officials were particularly interested in knowing which nonverbal tests would be most appropriate to use.

personal hygiene, and childrearing. Ellis Island even had a library with reading materials in several languages.

Despite such amenities, for many immigrants held at Ellis Island, being detained seemed like being jailed. This was in part because of set visiting hours, which were limited. Detainees could receive visitors on Tuesdays and Thursdays. This restriction was not lifted until the 1930s. Another concern was separating family members. Because men were held in one area and women and children in another, families were split up. This added stress to a situation that was already very challenging.

Poor Conditions

Another issue detainees faced was poor living conditions. Overcrowding increased the likelihood of areas being dirty and unsanitary. This applied to more than only the detention areas. The kitchen and dining room were often dirty. Sometimes it was because immigrants left messes behind, and sometimes it was because overcrowding kept workers from doing a thorough job of cleaning.

Overcrowding became a problem as the number of immigrants passing through the station grew.

Williams described the poor conditions:

When there are from 800 to 1,000 persons packed into these quarters . . . the conditions are indescribably bad. The toilet facilities too, are inadequate and the ventilating system is incapable of carrying off the foul air.[5]

Food was another issue. Ellis Island sometimes provided few options in terms of eating. In 1907, the site's busiest year, there were up to 2,000 detainees each day, and they all needed to eat.[6] Frank Martocci worked as an inspector and interpreter at Ellis Island. He described a scene in which one worker brought out slices of rye bread and another carried a large bucket of prunes. The workers gave detainees a slice of bread with a ladleful of prunes on it. One of them said, "Here! Now go eat!" Martocci said of the scene, "The poor wretches had to obey, though they didn't know where to go. They moved along, their harassed faces full of fear."[7]

Williams's collection includes a photo of a group of immigrants eating in a dining area.

ELLIS ISLAND'S BUSIEST YEAR

The year 1907 was Ellis Island's busiest. The total number of ships that arrived that year was 3,818.[8] From them, 1,004,756 people went ashore on the island. Of those, 195,540 were detained. Of those detentions, 121,737 were simply a matter of waiting for a relative to get them or waiting for money, which could take hours or days.[9]

Levick took the image. It shows women and children who are dressed meagerly, packed on benches at long tables.

Deported

Of the millions of immigrants who sought to pass through Ellis Island, only a small percentage were denied. Immigration officials turned away approximately 2 percent of arrivals at Ellis Island in 1911, the year of the highest percentage of deportations. This totaled approximately 13,000 people.[10] One challenge families faced was that if one child could not gain entry, officials denied entry to the child's entire family. This was because children were not allowed to travel alone.

In the early 1900s, the US government continued to focus on immigration and add to its list of undesirables through legislation. For example, the Immigration Act of 1903 singled out anarchists, beggars, and epileptics. In addition, by 1907, laws also made the shipping companies responsible for taking deportees back to their homelands. This was not enforced just for new arrivals. It was also in effect for immigrants living in the country for up to three years. As a result, shipping companies made the boarding process tougher. Shipping agents,

who represented the companies and sold passengers tickets, asked more questions to provide more details to US officials. By being stricter and making getting a ticket more difficult, the companies hoped to increase the likelihood their passengers would be admitted into the United States. The companies wanted to avoid having to pay for any immigrants the United States decided to deport.

Fighting Shipping Companies

Williams also went after the shipping companies. Because the companies were supposed to inspect immigrants on their ships before they landed at Ellis Island, Williams expected arrivals to pass his inspection. He discovered the contrary. During his first week as commissioner, he contacted a French shipping company to complain. The company had noted on its manifests that all the immigrants aboard were in good physical condition. But physicians at Ellis

LONG-TERM RESIDENTS DEPORTED

The United States did not hesitate to deport immigrants, even years after they arrived in the country. The legal limit for these deportations was typically a few years. But in 1919, exceptions to this made headlines. Government officials detained 249 Russian immigrants and then sent them back to Russia.[11] The US government was concerned these people were radicals. At the time, people were afraid of the spread of Communism. Two of the immigrants sent back to Russia were longtime residents of the United States. Emma Goldman had been in the country since 1885. Alexander Berkman had been there since 1888.

Island discovered these arrivals had a variety of medical issues, including blindness, clubfoot, hernias, and hunched backs.

There were other problems with the shipping companies. Aware that those in steerage were inspected much more thoroughly than those in first- and second-class cabins, shipping companies sometimes tried to sneak sick immigrants into the country by transporting them in one of the better classes. Doing so would allow the companies to make money. One example of this happened with the Red Star Line International Navigation Company. One of its ships, the *Southwark*, transported a family of seven immigrants. Six family members were belowdecks in steerage. They were healthy. The seventh had favus, a scalp disease that made a person inadmissible, and traveled in second class.

On May 28, 1902, Williams wrote a letter to Lawson Sandford, who was a lawyer for multiple shipping companies. He made his stance on the matter of cabin classes clear: "I shall hereafter treat all first cabin manifests in precisely the same way I treat steerage manifests."[12] In another instance involving passengers with favus, Williams contacted the ship's owners and focused on their health screening. Williams wrote, "A case of this sort merely goes to show that your system of medical inspection is far removed from what it should be."[13] In an effort to get shipping

companies to do a better job of inspecting immigrants, Williams imposed fines. Between

May 1902 and May 1903, he collected $6,560 from shipping companies for failing to inspect

immigrants properly.[14]

CHAPTER SIX

The Workers of Ellis Island

One Levick image shows employees at work at a Board of Special Inquiry hearing for an immigrant.

Processing the millions of people who arrived at Ellis Island each year required many employees in a variety of roles. In 1903, the second year Williams was on the job as commissioner, Ellis Island had 350 employees. They were assigned to one of 17 areas, such as medical or janitorial.[1] Sometimes, the number of personnel ballooned to as many as 500 and included additional inspectors, doctors, nurses, interpreters, and aid workers.[2] The staff also included clerks who worked with statistics, garbage collectors, handymen, and maids. These employees were crucial to the island's functioning, but they generally did not have face-to-face contact with immigrants.

Inspectors

Inspectors met with immigrants to interview them. All immigrants were interviewed. Some were interviewed while still on their ships. The rest were interviewed at Ellis Island itself.

An inspector had to determine two things. First, he had to make sure the immigrant was the person he or she claimed to be. This meant comparing the person's answers during the interview to the information on the ship's manifest. Second, the inspector had to determine if the person met US immigration rules or would end up relying on the government for aid. The government also specified certain groups of people as unwanted. They included anarchists, convicted criminals, and polygamists.

NO FAVORITISM IN HIRING AND PROMOTION

As commissioner, Williams refused to hire or promote people who did not deserve to work in a particular job. This was not the practice of his predecessors, who often took part in cronyism, the practice of hiring and promoting people because of who they knew rather than for doing good work. Shortly after becoming commissioner, Williams received a letter from Thomas Platt. In it, the New York senator asked Williams to promote a man named Samuel Samsom from gateman to inspector. Williams refused. In his response to Platt, Williams wrote that Samsom "is not fitted either by temperament or training for a position much above that held by him now."[3] Williams revamped the island's corrupt system of hiring and promoting workers. The new system was based much more on job performance.

Doctors, Interpreters, and Clerks

The doctors who worked on Ellis Island were uniformed members of the US Public Health Service. These personnel went by the title "surgeon." They worked in several areas of the inspection process. Some did their work on newly arrived ships, inspecting passengers in the first and second classes. Others worked in the inspection lines, examining the arrivals who had traveled in steerage. Doctors also worked in Ellis Island's hospitals, helping the immigrants who were placed there.

Some doctors at Ellis Island struggled with their work. They felt being assigned there was punishment for doing a bad job somewhere else. The only medical work on the island that was considered good—at least to some physicians—was the hospital. There, the immigrants believed the doctors were trying to be helpful. Being a doctor on the inspection line, however, could be physically and emotionally draining. Dealing with the constant influx of people could be overwhelming, especially when many new arrivals did not speak English and some were in dire circumstances, arriving penniless and dirty.

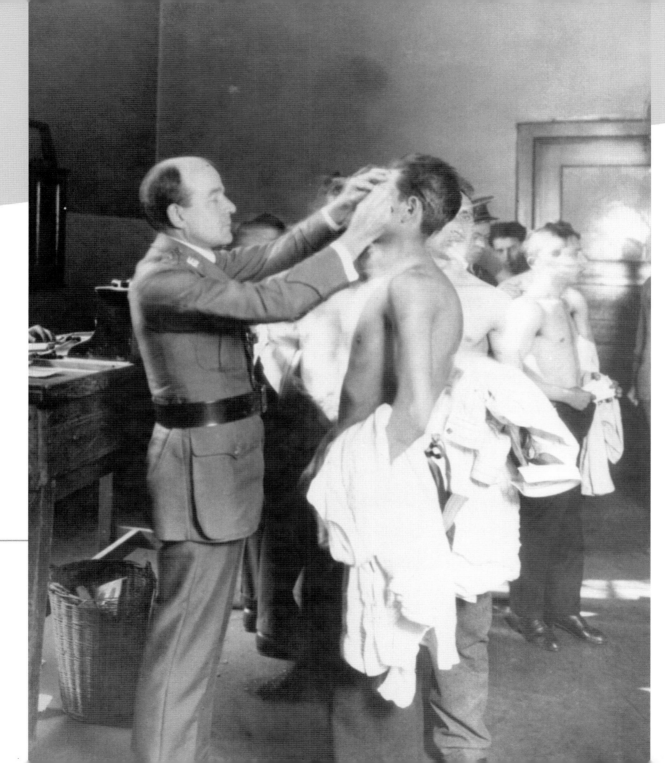

Doctors examine a line of immigrants for signs of communicable diseases.

Due to frequent language barriers, interpreters played an important role at Ellis Island. They helped new arrivals communicate with inspectors, doctors, and other workers on the island. Immigrants had access to interpreters at every stage of the inspection process at which they might need one. In 1911, interpreters speaking 37 languages were available to aid immigrants.[4] However, interpreters were not always highly skilled. Some were not fluent in both speaking and writing the language they interpreted.

Clerks dealt with paperwork at Ellis Island, and there was a tremendous amount of it. Clerks worked with ships' logs, which contained information about the passengers. Clerks also maintained immigrants' files, as well as files regarding detention and deportation. They did other record keeping as well. Dozens of clerks and stenographers worked at the site. One of Levick's photos shows immigrants being registered at the Great Hall. Clerks sit on one side

GIVING PRAISE

As commissioner, Williams was a strict manager, but he did not point out only faulty behavior. He also praised employees. Fiorello La Guardia, who went on to serve as mayor of New York City from 1933 to 1945, worked as an interpreter at Ellis Island from 1907 to 1910. In 1910, Williams recommended La Guardia for promotion, writing, "Mr. La Guardia is energetic, intelligent and familiar with a number of foreign languages. Against him there may be said that he is inclined to be peppery; that with some of the Board [of Special Inquiry] Members, he is inclined to the argumentative, but . . . it is not a defect of the first order. . . . I think that his abilities place him in the higher grade of interpreters. . . . I, therefore, suggest his regular promotion to the $1,380 grade."[5]

of a long table, papers spread out in front of them. Immigrants sit or stand on the other side of the table, their suitcase or other luggage on the floor nearby, quite possibly containing all they own. Thanks to his photographs, Sherman is perhaps Ellis Island's best known clerk.

Other Workers

In addition to managing government employees, Williams also kept an eye on other people who worked at the site but did not report to him. These included concessionaires, the people who ran concessions, which included exchanging money, handling baggage, and selling food. The concessionaires were employees of the companies that had contracts with the government to work at Ellis Island.

One dishonest concessionaire Williams caught worked as a currency exchanger. When changing immigrants' currencies to US currency, he gave them less than they were owed. Williams said of the man, "One can only have contempt for a man who will unjustly enrich himself at the expense of the ignorant and helpless immigrants."[6]

NAME CHANGES

A long-standing myth holds that workers at Ellis Island changed some immigrants' names, Americanizing foreign names into versions Americans could more easily manage. In reality, Ellis Island's inspectors were charged with verifying information, not changing it. As immigrants made their way through processing, they had to answer questions based on information in ship records. The person who created a ship's manifest perhaps misspelled an immigrant's name. If an Ellis Island inspector altered a name, it would be to correct the spelling.

The real source for most of these name changes is the immigrants themselves. Immigrants who did change their names did so for various reasons. Some chose a name that was more American. That would help them fit in better in their new neighborhoods and country, or it might help if the person had a business. The right-sounding name might attract customers.

Some of these new Americans who changed their names did so officially. However, filing paperwork for a name change was not required in New York in the early 1900s. Some immigrants simply started using a new name, and there is no official record of the person's original and new names.

Immigrants registered with inspectors upon arrival in the facility's main hall.

Newly admitted immigrants waited to exchange their money for US currency before leaving the island.

Success

Williams recognized early on that to improve the immigrant experience at Ellis Island and restore the site's reputation, he would have to improve its policies and practices. But changing the way things were done would not be good enough. He had to get rid of those workers who did not meet his high standards and reinforce those standards by pointing out to workers when they failed to reach the bar he set.

Williams's changes made a difference at Ellis Island. In December 1903, President Roosevelt acknowledged the improvements in a speech to Congress in which he discussed the state of the country. Roosevelt said, "During the last two years the immigration service of New York has been greatly improved, and the corruption and inefficiency which formerly obtained there have been eradicated."[7]

By 1905, immigrants were eating better food and experiencing better conditions, including improved treatment by workers. Williams had done what Roosevelt had asked of him. He decided to quit his job as commissioner. He submitted his letter of resignation in January 1905. Roosevelt was pleased with Williams's work as commissioner and praised him:

I feel that you have rendered a service of real and high importance to the whole nation in your management of the office under you. . . . You have set a standard of unceasing industry, of untiring energy, of high administrative ability and of single-minded devotion to duty which your successor will find it difficult to equal, no matter how good a man he may be.[8]

A SUPPORTIVE PRESIDENT

As commissioner of Ellis Island, Williams had the full support of Theodore Roosevelt. The president did not simply appoint Williams and wait to see what would happen. Rather, Roosevelt participated in the overhaul of Ellis Island's reputation. In June 1902, just two months after Williams became commissioner, Roosevelt sent a letter requesting the names of workers Williams believed were part of the problem at the immigration processing center. Roosevelt wrote why he wanted the list of names: "I wish to have it on hand for use in making other people understand that I am perfectly ready to fight if they insist upon having a fight over this matter."[9]

CHAPTER SEVEN

Interim and Return

After leaving his post at Ellis Island in 1905, Williams spoke out about immigration. He had been a supporter of restrictions on immigrants and wrote an article on the subject that appeared in the *Journal of Social Science*. In it, Williams said,

> *I am convinced that a certain minority of the present immigration is undesirable, and that, if some means can be found to prevent this undesirable minority from coming here, not only will we be greatly benefitted, but we are likely to attract more immigrants of the better kind.*[1]

Williams left Ellis Island in 1905, but he would not be gone for long.

He went on to say that one-quarter of immigrants who were admitted were actually "not wanted," writing they were "the undesirable minority."[2]

Becoming Commissioner Again

While Williams was busy advocating immigration restriction, Ellis Island was returning to its old, corrupt ways. Unhappy with what was going on, President William Howard Taft offered Williams the job of commissioner again. Williams accepted, and he resumed the post in May 1909.

During his second term as commissioner, Williams again set out to fight corruption. He also focused on restricting immigrants. As did many restrictionists, Williams believed earlier groups that came from Northern Europe were

more desirable than those from Eastern and Southern Europe. In an interview with the *New York Times*, he said these earlier immigrants were "as good as the new immigrants are bad."[3] With federal laws on his side that allowed exclusion for reasons ranging from physical and mental health to criminal history to a likelihood of needing government assistance, Williams worked to carry out his own agenda. In a yearly report, Williams wrote that immigrants from Southern and Eastern Europe "have very low standards of living, possess filthy habits, and are of an ignorance which passes belief."[4]

Williams held strong personal beliefs about immigration, but he still worked to follow federal immigration legislation. As a lawyer, he held laws in high regard. That meant he operated within them. As a result, he had to allow entry to some immigrants he otherwise would ban. A week into his second term as commissioner, he gave the employees of Ellis Island the following message:

> It is necessary that the standard of inspection at Ellis Island be raised. Notice hereof is given publicly in order that intending immigrants may be advised before embarkation that our immigration laws will be strictly enforced, and that those who are unable to measure up to its requirements may not waste their time or money in coming here, only to encounter the hardships of deportation.[5]

The $25 Rule

In 1909, Williams specified that immigrants should have at least $25. The commissioner believed this would keep them from needing charity. In 2016, that requirement would be approximately $630.

Williams's new rule made it difficult for impoverished people to pass through Ellis Island.

Immigrants felt the effect of Williams's new rule immediately. The day it went into effect, inspectors detained 215 of the 301 passengers on a single ship for not meeting the monetary minimum.[6] Most of those arrivals were allowed into the country, but only after they could sufficiently prove they would not require public assistance.

Immigrants protested. Williams did not care. He said in response to the protests, "I have enforced the laws. Why shouldn't I? That's what I am here for."[7] Some Americans wrote angry letters. Some newspapers also addressed the issue. The *New York World* stated,

In this country a $25 rule would have kept the great West a wilderness; would have preserved the Great American Desert to this day; would have deprived the Pacific Coast of its forty-nine and the railroad builders; would have kept Benjamin Franklin out of Philadelphia.[8]

Williams's superiors soon overturned his $25 rule.

Williams showed his strict nature when he served on boards of special inquiry and heard individual cases for being allowed to enter the

MEDICAL CERTIFICATE REQUIRED

The Immigration Act of 1907 established a new requirement for immigrants. They had to obtain a medical certificate that proclaimed whether they were "mentally or physically defective" to the extent that it would "affect [their] ability to earn a living."[9] This requirement highlighted the idea of becoming a public charge. If an immigrant could not earn a living, he or she would likely need public assistance.

country. In one instance, Williams considered the case of a woman and her little boy, who was deaf and mute. Williams wanted the pair deported. The reason he gave the mother was that "her child will always be physically defective."[10]

A Second Resignation

As Williams's control over who entered the country through Ellis Island seemed to grow tighter and tighter, some groups took action. Foreign-language newspapers were especially critical of Williams. Several German-language newspapers across the country printed editorials against him. Some of the papers referred to him as a czar, thinking he behaved as a ruthless dictator.

Finally, in 1913, Williams resigned a second time. Once again, he would leave behind policies

BOARDS OF SPECIAL INQUIRY

The 1891 law that made immigration the responsibility of the federal government also established boards of special inquiry. Immigrants who were detained could go before a board of special inquiry and state their case for entry into the United States. These boards had three to four members. These were not courts, but they acted similarly to a court, with members hearing testimony from people who knew the immigrant requesting the proceeding. An interpreter and a social service worker might also attend and assist. During the hearing, the board members would ask the immigrant and his or her witnesses questions about the immigrant and about the reasons for that person's detainment.

In 1910, during Williams's second, stricter term as commissioner, boards of special inquiry heard 70,829 cases.[11] The most common issue immigrants challenged was becoming a public charge. On one occasion, the board made a single mother with four children swear on a bible that none of her children "would ever become a burden on the country."[12]

A photo from Williams's collection shows a man, possibly Williams, looking out from the island in 1913.

and procedures that made immigrant processing on Ellis Island more efficient and less corrupt than it had been before he arrived. Ellis Island's heyday would soon end, however, with the US government clamping down on immigrants more and more. But it would live on, too, thanks to Williams's interest in documenting his time as commissioner.

CORRUPTION: THE DEPORTED RETURN

Immigrants whom officials deported sometimes made it into the United States. This was one form of corruption Williams was determined to fight as commissioner. In 1904, he noted how detainees placed on ships to be returned to their homelands escaped by bribing the ship's workers: "The temptation to connive to escape, especially if the person ordered deported has money and friends to go to in this city, is very great."[13]

The problem continued for several years. In 1910, during his second term as commissioner, Williams filed corruption charges against the Hellenic Transatlantic Steam Navigation Company. Crew members had accepted money to get sick immigrants into the United States. Fifteen employees of the company went to jail.

CHAPTER EIGHT

Ellis Island after Williams

A few years after Williams left his job at Ellis Island a second time, the US government began to enact legislation to further limit the number of immigrants entering the United States. Overall immigration numbers started to decline in the late 1920s. Because these laws dramatically affected immigration, they had a major effect on Ellis Island.

The downturn cut down on the amount of work at Ellis Island. It also decreased the site's prominence. With that, the office of the commissioner also lost prominence. The number of immigrants

A group of immigrants prepares to leave Ellis Island behind and enter the United States after passing their inspections.

entering the United States dropped further in the 1940s, during World War II (1939–1945). During the war, the government used the site as a detention center, holding enemy aliens there.

The shift in transportation also played a part in the decline of Ellis Island as a site for processing immigrants. As the mode of arrival moved from sea to air, the historic site became obsolete.

More than 100 years after Williams served as commissioner of Ellis Island, immigration continues to be a major topic of discussion among Americans and politicians. Immigration in the United States is now a complex system with different tracks for entry, including having an immediate family member who is a US citizen, having a job, and being a refugee or an asylum-seeker. The US government limits the number of people who can enter the United States each year in each category of the immigration system. The government also limits

ELLIS ISLAND'S ABANDONED BUILDINGS

The Great Hall was the center of Ellis Island, but the island had more than two dozen other buildings. When the site reopened as a tourist attraction, many of the immigration processing center's buildings remained abandoned. The south side of the island is home to 29 buildings. Until 2014, they were off limits to visitors. That year, Save Ellis Island Inc. started the Hard Hat Tour tourist program. Visitors can now explore the buildings, though they must wear hard hats due to the buildings' physical state.

the number of people from a
single country to no more than
7 percent of the total number of
immigrants.[1]

According to US Customs
and Border Protection, almost
one million people enter the
United States every day.[2] US
Customs and Border Protection
officers inspect everyone who
arrives. This includes reviewing
paperwork each person is
required to provide. It varies by
country of origin. Paperwork includes a customs form on which a person provides information
such as his or her name, passport number, and country of residence, and whether he or she is
bringing in items such as food or plants.

Airplanes later replaced ships for crossings of
the Atlantic Ocean.

Closing the Facility

Even after the war, immigration at Ellis Island did not increase. Finally, in 1954, after more than 60 years of use, the US Immigration and Naturalization Service closed the facility. But the site would eventually reopen in a new role.

In 1965, President Lyndon B. Johnson issued a presidential proclamation that made the island part of the National Park System. But the location did not open to the public for more than two decades. In 1990, Ellis Island once again opened; this time, it was a museum focused on immigration. Today, the site has three floors of exhibits. Visitors can view belongings of some of the immigrants that made their way to Ellis Island. Other items in the museum's collection include historic photos, such as those by Sherman, as well as newspaper clippings and political cartoons on the topic of Ellis Island and immigration.

The site is home to the American Family Immigration History Center, which conducts research. The center houses records on more than 22 million people, including immigrants, ship passengers, and ship crews.[3] Members of the public can search through these records.

Williams's Collection

When Williams left Ellis Island and the job of commissioner the second time, he did not retire. He took a position at the New York City Department of Water Supply. His title there was the same as at Ellis Island: commissioner. Just as he had done with immigration processing, Williams cleaned up the water department. He tried to lower the cost of utilities to residents. He also proposed changing the city's lights from gas to electric, but officials rejected his idea.

A BOOK OF SHERMAN'S PHOTOGRAPHS

In 2005, Aperture Foundation published a book of Sherman's photographs. Titled *Augustus F. Sherman: Ellis Island Portraits, 1905–1920*, the book includes images not part of Williams's collection. The book begins with a historical essay by Peter Mesenhöller, a cultural anthropologist who specializes in early still photography and immigration studies. Mesenhöller discusses immigration at Ellis Island when Sherman worked there, provides some biographical information about the photographer, and considers Sherman's photos in the context of other photographers.

Williams worked at the water department until the end of 1917. Next, he took a contract military job, serving as a lieutenant colonel in the Ordnance Department of the US Army from 1918 to 1919. He worked in the Procurement Division, which obtained supplies for the army. His office was in Washington, DC. After that, he decided to practice law again. Williams died in 1947. He never married.

In September 1947, Williams's estate donated a collection of items to the New York Public Library. Among them were ten boxes and a large folder containing photos and documents Williams had collected while at Ellis Island.

Williams's Ellis Island collection is varied. He saved letters, notices, and reports. He collected watercolor sketches in addition to his photographs. He also kept scrapbooks. The diligent commissioner was also diligent in recording history. Today, people can view items from the collection online. In January 2016, the library made more than 180,000 digitized items available on its website, including artifacts from Williams, such as photographs.[4]

Ellis Island was the nation's primary location for processing immigrants for only a

ANALYZING SHERMAN'S PHOTOGRAPHS

In 2008, Alan G. Artner, a critic for the *Chicago Tribune*, critiqued Sherman's Ellis Island images as artistic works. The images had been on display at the DePaul University Art Museum. Artner wrote, "What might have looked fine at a library or historical society proved disappointing at best when seen in places that set up aesthetic expectations."[5]

The response of Peter Mesenhöller to Sherman's photos in 2005 was very different. The cultural anthropologist viewed the images at the Ellis Island Immigration Museum. He said, "I immediately got stunned by the dignity, the pride, the self-confidence. It was totally different from the usual image we have of the huddled masses."[6] Perhaps Diana Edkins, a member of the Aperture Foundation, which published a book of Sherman's photographs, explained the appeal of Sherman's work best: "[Sherman] didn't impose his own feeling on these people. He really showed it in a very stripped-down documentary-like way."[7]

few decades. Those years of operation were a critical time in the history of US immigration, its processes, and its laws. For the millions of people who made their way to America, it took all they had to get here. They survived terrible trips across the Atlantic Ocean, followed by questioning and rigorous examinations. Most entered the country. Some were sent home. Thanks to William Williams, a record exists of what they looked like, along with the buildings and grounds they saw as they took their first steps on American soil, all with the hope of making this foreign country home.

ON GUARD —

World, July 1

HERE THEY COME!

Commissioner of Immigration William Williams.

Common Sense and Deep Knowledg of Human Nature Are Applied in Weeding the Unfit from the Fit Among the Immigrants at Ellis Island.

Williams's collection includes a variety of newspaper clippings covering his tenure as commissioner.

1

2

3

4

5

PHOTOGRAPHING ELLIS ISLAND

1. ## The Processing Building

   Edwin Levick captured this image of the immigration processing building in the early 1900s. The sight was experienced by millions of foreigners who arrived at Ellis Island.

2. ## Family from Hungary

   Williams kept this image from the February 12, 1905, issue of the *New York Times*. Taken by Augustus Sherman, it shows the meager state of many who arrived at Ellis Island. This family from Hungary, labeled as gypsies, was deported.

3. ## The Great Hall

   This photo from Williams's collection gives a sense of the wait immigrants had to go through when being processed on Ellis Island.

4. ## Ferryboat

   William Williams kept this photo from the early 1900s of a ferryboat with immigrants. It shows one of the steps of the immigration process—after arriving by ship, immigrants had to travel by ferry or barge to Ellis Island.

5. ## Dutch Children

   Even the youngest of arrivals were often dressed in traditional attire of their homelands, such as the wooden shoes worn by these Dutch children.

Quote

"I immediately got stunned by the dignity, the pride, the self-confidence. It was totally different from the usual image we have of the huddled masses."

—*Cultural anthropologist Peter Mesenhöller on Augustus Sherman's photos*

GLOSSARY

anarchist
A person who believes countries should not have governments.

asylum-seeker
Someone who has fled his or her country and cannot return to it for fear of harm or death and is seeking protection from another country.

emigrate
To leave one's place of residence or country to live elsewhere.

gallows
A structure used to put people to death by hanging.

garb
A style of dress; fashion; type of clothing.

immigration
The process of moving to a new country.

landfill
An area of land created or built up by layering earth and trash.

manifest
The official list of items and people on a ship.

polygamist
Someone who is married to two or more people at the same time.

public assistance

Aid from the government or other organizations that a person uses because he or she cannot support himself or herself.

Puritan

A member of a Protestant group in England and New England during the 1500s and 1600s that was against the Church of England.

refugee

Someone who has fled his or her country and cannot return to it for fear of harm or death; the person has not yet entered the United States.

steerage

The area of a ship where people with the cheapest tickets stayed.

stenographer

A person who can use shorthand to take notes or write letters as someone dictates to them.

trachoma

A contagious eye disease caused by bacteria that causes inflammation and often causes blindness if not treated.

ADDITIONAL RESOURCES

Selected Bibliography

Bayor, Ronald H. *Encountering Ellis Island: How European Immigrants Entered America*. Baltimore, MD: Johns Hopkins UP, 2014. Print.

Bergquist, James M. *Daily Life in Immigrant America, 1820–1870*. Westport, CT: Greenwood, 2008. Print.

Cannato, Vincent J. *American Passage: The History of Ellis Island*. New York: Harper, 2009. Print.

Further Readings

Mesenhöller, Peter. *Augustus F. Sherman: Ellis Island Portraits, 1905–1920*. New York: Aperture, 2005. Print.

Osborne, Linda Barrett. *This Land Is Our Land: A History of American Immigration*. New York: Abrams, 2016. Print.

Wilkes, Stephen. *Ellis Island: Ghosts of Freedom*. New York: Norton, 2006. Print.

Websites

To learn more about Defining Images, visit **abdobooklinks.com**. These links are routinely monitored and updated to provide the most current information available.

For More Information

For more information on this subject, contact or visit the following organizations:

CASTLE CLINTON

26 Wall Street
New York, NY 10005
212-344-7220
https://www.nps.gov/cacl/index.htm

Explore this site that processed eight million immigrants in 34 years prior to the opening of Ellis Island.

ELLIS ISLAND MUSEUM OF IMMIGRATION

Ellis Island
New York, NY 10004
212-363-3200
https://www.nps.gov/elis/index.htm

View the 30-minute award-winning documentary *Island of Hope, Island of Tears*, view exhibits about the immigrants who passed through Ellis Island, and take a 90-minute guided tour of the island's south side, where the hospital is located.

STATUE OF LIBERTY

Liberty Island
New York, NY 10004
212-363-3200
https://www.nps.gov/stli/index.htm

Explore the Statue of Liberty, the beacon of hope in New York Harbor, including the museum in the statue's pedestal and the statue's crown.

SOURCE NOTES

CHAPTER 1. TAKING CHARGE

1. Vincent J. Cannato. *American Passage: The History of Ellis Island*. New York: Harper, 2009. Print. 139.

2. "Ellis Island." *History*. A+E Television Networks, 2016. Web. 1 May 2016.

CHAPTER 2. IMMIGRATION TO AMERICA

1. "Jamestown Colony." *History*. A+E Television Networks, 2016. Web. 1 May 2016.

2. Kevin Hillstrom. *The Dream of America: Immigration, 1870–1920*. Detroit, MI: Omnigraphics, 2009. Print. 14–15.

3. Ibid.

4. "Irish Immigrants: Early Nineteenth Century." *Immigration to the United States*. Immigration to the United States, 2015. Web. 24 Oct. 2016.

5. Kevin Hillstrom. *The Dream of America: Immigration, 1870–1920*. Detroit, MI: Omnigraphics, 2009. Print. 19–20.

6. Ibid. 27.

7. "Ellis Island." *History*. A+E Television Networks, 2016. Web. 1 May 2016.

8. "America's First Immigration Center." *CastleGarden.org*. The Battery Foundation, n.d. Web. 24 Oct. 2016.

9. Kevin Hillstrom. *The Dream of America: Immigration, 1870–1920*. Detroit, MI: Omnigraphics, 2009. Print. 44.

10. Kathryn Shattuck. "When Old and New World Met in a Camera Flash." *New York Times*. New York Times Company, 6 Aug. 2005. Web. 30 May 2016.

CHAPTER 3. THE JOURNEY TO ELLIS ISLAND

1. "Ellis Island." *History*. A+E Television Networks, 2016. Web. 1 May 2016.

2. Ibid.

3. Ibid.

4. Ibid.

5. "Spaces and Places: America's Cultural Landscapes." *National Park Service*. National Park Service, 3 July 2012. Web. 2 Oct. 2016.

6. "Ellis Island." *History*. A+E Television Networks, 2016. Web. 1 May 2016.

7. Kevin Hillstrom. *The Dream of America: Immigration, 1870–1920*. Detroit, MI: Omnigraphics, 2009. Print. 36.

8. Ibid. 37.

9. Ronald H. Bayor. *Encountering Ellis Island: How European Immigrants Entered America*. Baltimore, MD: Johns Hopkins UP, 2014. Print. 22.

10. Kevin Hillstrom. *The Dream of America: Immigration, 1870–1920*. Detroit, MI: Omnigraphics, 2009. Print. 36.

11. Hannah Miller. "Keeping a Nation's Gates: William Williams, Ellis Island, and Immigration Regulation in Early Twentieth Century America." *MA Thesis*. Georgetown U, 2014. Print. 29.

12. Vincent J. Cannato. *American Passage: The History of Ellis Island*. New York: Harper, 2009. Print. 142.

13. Ibid. 150.

14. Kevin Hillstrom. *The Dream of America: Immigration, 1870–1920*. Detroit, MI: Omnigraphics, 2009. Print. 139.

CHAPTER 4. ISLAND OF HOPE, ISLAND OF TEARS

1. Ronald H. Bayor. *Encountering Ellis Island: How European Immigrants Entered America*. Baltimore, MD: Johns Hopkins UP, 2014. Print. 27.

2. Kevin Hillstrom. *The Dream of America: Immigration 1870–1920*. Detroit, MI: Omnigraphics, 2009. Print. 4.

3. Ronald H. Bayor. *Encountering Ellis Island: How European Immigrants Entered America*. Baltimore, MD: Johns Hopkins UP, 2014. Print. 43.

4. Ibid. 98–99.

5. Hannah Miller. "Keeping a Nation's Gates: William Williams, Ellis Island, and Immigration Regulation in Early Twentieth Century America." *MA Thesis*. Georgetown U, 2014. Print. 40–41.

6. Vincent J. Cannato. *American Passage: The History of Ellis Island*. New York: Harper, 2009. Print. 140.

7. Hannah Miller. "Keeping a Nation's Gates: William Williams, Ellis Island, and Immigration Regulation in Early Twentieth Century America." *MA Thesis*. Georgetown U, 2014. Print. 34.

8. Peter Mesenhöller. *Augustus F. Sherman: Ellis Island Portraits, 1905–1920*. New York: Aperture, 2005. Print. 9.

9. Vincent J. Cannato. *American Passage: The History of Ellis Island*. New York: Harper, 2009. Print. 140–141.

10. Ibid. 141.

11. Ibid.

CHAPTER 5. DETAINED, DEPORTED

1. Vincent J. Cannato. *American Passage: The History of Ellis Island*. New York: Harper, 2009. Print. 195.

2. Ronald H. Bayor. *Encountering Ellis Island: How European Immigrants Entered America*. Baltimore, MD: Johns Hopkins UP, 2014. Print. 82.

3. "People and Events: Immigration and Deportation at Ellis Island." *PBS: American Experience: Emma Goldman*. PBS Online, 2004. Web. 11 May 2016.

4. Ronald H. Bayor. *Encountering Ellis Island: How European Immigrants Entered America*. Baltimore, MD: Johns Hopkins UP, 2014. Print. 86.

5. Ibid. 85.

6. Ibid.

7. Ibid.

8. Ibid. 27.

9. Ibid. 39.

10. Ibid. 40.

11. Ibid. 81.

12. Hannah Miller. "Keeping a Nation's Gates: William Williams, Ellis Island, and Immigration Regulation in Early Twentieth Century America." *MA Thesis*. Georgetown U, 2014. Print. 35.

13. Ibid.

14. Vincent J. Cannato. *American Passage: The History of Ellis Island*. New York: Harper, 2009. Print. 140.

CHAPTER 6. THE WORKERS OF ELLIS ISLAND

1. Ronald H. Bayor. *Encountering Ellis Island: How European Immigrants Entered America*. Baltimore, MD: Johns Hopkins UP, 2014. Print. 103.

2. "Ellis Island: People: The Workers of Ellis Island." *National Park Service*. National Park Service, n.d. Web. 6 May 2016.

3. Vincent J. Cannato. *American Passage: The History of Ellis Island*. New York: Harper, 2009. Print. 140.

4. Ronald H. Bayor. *Encountering Ellis Island: How European Immigrants Entered America*. Baltimore, MD: Johns Hopkins UP, 2014. Print. 43.

5. "Ellis Island: Interpreter." *National Park Service*. National Park Service, n.d. Web. 22 Oct. 2016.

6. Hannah Miller. "Keeping a Nation's Gates: William Williams, Ellis Island, and Immigration Regulation in Early Twentieth Century America." *MA Thesis*. Georgetown U, 2014. Print. 38.

7. "Theodore Roosevelt: Third Annual Message." *The American Presidency Project*. University of California, San Diego, 2016. Web. 22 Oct. 2016.

8. Hannah Miller. "Keeping a Nation's Gates: William Williams, Ellis Island, and Immigration Regulation in Early Twentieth Century America." *MA Thesis*. Georgetown U, 2014. Print. 42.

9. Ibid. 28.

CHAPTER 7. INTERIM AND RETURN

1. Hannah Miller. "Keeping a Nation's Gates: William Williams, Ellis Island, and Immigration Regulation in Early Twentieth Century America." *MA Thesis*. Georgetown U, 2014. Print. 46–47.

2. Vincent J. Cannato. *American Passage: The History of Ellis Island*. New York: Harper, 2009. Print. 193.

3. Ibid. 194.

4. Vincent J. Cannato, "Coming to America: Ellis Island and New York City." *History Now*. Gilder Lehrman Institute of American History, n.d. Web. 13 June 2016.

5. Vincent J. Cannato. *American Passage: The History of Ellis Island*. New York: Harper, 2009. Print. 194.

6. Ibid. 196.

7. Ibid. 197.

8. Hannah Miller. "Keeping a Nation's Gates: William Williams, Ellis Island, and Immigration Regulation in Early Twentieth Century America." *MA Thesis*. Georgetown U, 2014. Print. 53.

9. Ibid. 54.

10. Ibid. 59.

11. Ronald H. Bayor. *Encountering Ellis Island: How European Immigrants Entered America*. Baltimore, MD: Johns Hopkins UP, 2014. Print. 66.

12. Ibid. 68.

13. Ibid. 115.

CHAPTER 8. ELLIS ISLAND AFTER WILLIAMS

1. "How the United States Immigration System Works." *American Immigration Council*. American Immigration Council, n.d. Web. 13 Nov. 2016.

2. "Travel." *US Customs and Border Protection*. US Department of Homeland Security, 4 Nov. 2016. Web. 14 Nov. 2016.

3. "Ellis Island: The Portal to America for 12 Million Immigrants from 1782 to 1924." *Ellis Island*. National Parks of New York Harbor Conservancy, 2016. Web. 24. Oct. 2016.

4. Camila Domonoske. "New York Public Library Makes 180,000 High-Res Images Available Online." *NPR*. NPR, 6 Jan. 2016. Web. 24 Oct. 2016.

5. Alan G. Artner. "Sherman's Ellis Island Portraits Tell Another Tale of Immigration." *Chicago Tribune*. Chicago Tribune, 24 Apr. 2008. Web. 30 May 2016.

6. Kathryn Shattuck. "When Old and New World Met in a Camera Flash." *New York Times*. New York Times Company, 6 Aug. 2005. Web. 30 May 2016.

7. Ibid.

INDEX

About the Author

Rebecca Rowell has worked on numerous books for young readers as an author and as an editor. Her writing includes titles about ancient India, Rachel Carson, John F. Kennedy, and the Louisiana Purchase. One of her favorite parts of writing is doing research and learning about all kinds of subjects. Rebecca has a master's degree in publishing and writing from Emerson College. She lives in Minneapolis, Minnesota.